A MAN SURVIVES

A MAN SURVIVES

Vladimir Maximov

Translated by Anselm Hollo

GROVE PRESS, INC.

NEW YORK

Copyright © 1963 by Grove Press, Inc.

Originally published as *Zhiv Shelovek* in *Oktyabr*, Moscow, 1962

All Rights Reserved

No part of this book may be reproduced, for any reason, by any means, including any method of photographic reproduction, without the permission of the publisher.

ISBN: 0-394-17865-3
Grove Press ISBN: 0-8021-0055-4

Library of Congress Catalog Card Number: 73-21010

First Evergreen Edition

First Printing

Manufactured in the United States of America

Distributed by Random House, Inc., New York

What is good is always present in our souls, and the soul is good; what is evil has been forced into it from outside.

—Tolstoy

1

My eyelids feel glued down, I have difficulty opening them: brilliant, cutting light is piercing my eyeballs. Circles—blue, green, and red—floating about, multiplying. Then, two faces coming through the filigree rainbow-patterns. One of them, a young face with high, Mongol cheekbones and wide-apart almond-shaped eyes: the other, an old face, crumpled by time, thin-lipped. Quiet, seemingly indifferent voices rustling above me.

—Kolya knows?

—But yes, I've told him.

—Just tell him straight . . . .

—Yes indeed, just tell him—and he'll think I'm trying to force myself on him! No, I'll have the child first, and then he can make up his mind.

—He's the father of that child.

—So he is. So, what?

—He has to marry you!

—Oh no he doesn't! Why should he? Out of pity? If he doesn't want to marry me, he can just leave me alone —I'll take care of the kid.

—My my, what a sense of honor you youngsters have . . . . But little sense otherwise! In my young days your father would have ripped your skirt to pieces, and set you down in a tanner's vat, on your bare back-side . . . .

—What a horrible blizzard . . . .

I can hear the wind now, raving and howling outside. From time to time it falls silent, then it comes rushing against the walls with renewed strength, crackling like dry peas against the windowpanes, or like somebody throwing fistfuls of gravel . . . . I can hear the hoarse obbligato of the generators through these snowy squalls, and the little ceiling lightbulb flickers to their rhythms, though almost imperceptibly.

—Our Sima is beside herself . . . . There he lies, a human being, waiting to be operated on, to be saved, and Ivan Antonovitch can't get away from Zaburovo!

—You're trembling! Is he going to lose his legs? But no! Oh no, no—God, forgive me!

I let my eyelids fall. This is the way I'm informed of my condition; well, I'm getting used to it. But where am I, and how did I get here? The last thing in my memory is a fall, fiery and endless . . . .

The words, crackling like dry leaves in my ear.

—Antonovitch isn't here. She has to take all the responsibility, no one else.

—It's almost forty versts* from Zaburovo. And in this weather—

—He's quite a young man still, though he's in a terrible state—

—That's what I've been saying. If only he doesn't lose his legs!

—He's probably been with some expedition. Those people always have beards . . . .

—Yes . . . .

The conversation fades, and the terrible meaning of a phrase penetrates into my consciousness: "If only he doesn't lose his legs." If that happens, it's the end of me. Can't make it without legs! I make an involuntary effort to get up—but the pain, echoing the memory of a bullet tearing through, immediately hurls me into a dizzying void.

---

* Verst: about two-thirds of a mile.

2

~~~~~~

I step out on the porch, my school bag under my arm. In front of me are these three steps—I know them by heart—and from them, dividing our courtyard in two, a well-swept brick path, leading to the gate. As always, as yesterday, thick smoke is rising from the chimneys and smokestacks, grown to different heights, which surround this flat town of ours, Yuzhnogorsk; as yesterday, the sounds and colors, familiar since childhood days, come flowing toward me from all sides. The cocks crowing, the wash hanging out on the lines above the fence, the fluffy poplar seeds spinning in the air. As yesterday, I'm now on my way to school, and I'll be going there for a long,

long time yet, all of three years. But I do know that something inside me has suddenly changed. I used to see myself as a small, almost insignificant part of these surroundings; today it seems as if I have been stricken by a violent blast of light and torn out of my habitual setting. Every single step, every breath seems charged with this sense of steadily approaching, irrevocable change. And it has in fact begun: last night my father was arrested and taken away ....

It had been inevitable, more or less. Last year these strange men came to stay in our house. Men with similar faces, similar voices even—broken and muted voices.

And another thing: their hands seemed to be trembling incessantly. These hands could grasp things, contract into fists, touch and turn objects, open knots—but they did everything violently, nervously, as if afraid of great heat in everything they touched. Then they started drinking vodka, rattling off gruesome curses, and my mother, huddling under her blanket, could only sigh and complain:

—Alexey, that is enough now, pity the poor children!

But my father would reply, making weary, defensive gestures—

—Come on, come on now, go to sleep.

And in the mornings he walked through the house, quietly and almost shamefacedly, looking at all of us with an anxious, apologetic stare.

Now that's all over. Three men came, in the small hours of the morning, waking up everybody except Galka, my youngest baby sister. She was still waiting for the glorious end of her morning dreams, from time to time pulling up and smoothing her covers, while the militiaman with the bovine expression leaned against the wall between the door and Galka's cot. The other two, in plain clothes, were busy with the contents of the closet and the chest of drawers, dividing the things into two separate piles, as if playing a game of even and odd numbers. When they were through, the taller pile was covered with my father's long underpants, with its rust stains from the iron buttons of his trousers, and on top of the smaller pile lay our family album, in its worn morocco covers. Inside it, I knew, were moldy, dried flowers and photographs "of all our clan down to the seventh generation," as my mother used to say . . . .

Then one of the plain-clothes men nodded his head at my father and said:

—Let's get going, Zarev!

But my father couldn't manage to get his foot into the shoe. The shoe kept jumping away like a live thing, as soon as his foot touched it. My mother was holding on to the wardrobe with both hands, gently shivering with her whole body. The most terrifying thing was that she didn't cry, didn't strike out against these men, that she only stood there, lost in that continuous trembling. But the most memorable image was that of the underpants with their iron button rust stains, and the family album, a corner of a yellow, faded photograph sticking out, with the fragment of a dedication: "For Fyenitchka, from her dear par . . . ."

A voice, familiar to the point of making my cheek muscles ache:

—Seryosha!

That's Zina, she sits next to me in school. She has a pair of rubbery pigtails, a freckled nose with slightly flattened nostrils and round eyes, with a perennially surprised expression at the bottom of them. Zina lives in the house across the road. That is why we always walk together, to school and back home again. But perhaps not only for that reason . . . . The other kids often tease us, call us "bride and groom"; when this happens, Zina just shrugs her bony, obstinate shoulders, and I, I start punching them in the face.

Now she is standing in front of me, hanging her head, the point of one shoe drawing slow zigzagging lines in the dust on the sidewalk.

—Mother says I shouldn't walk with you anymore.

I follow the lines of her drawing with a dull stare.

—Why's that?

—You should know.

—I see, yes.

I turn away from her and start walking off. She catches up with me, and from somewhere far away, it seems, her voice reaches my ears:

—But I'll still stay next to you in class, I give you my Pioneer's word!

Well, let her stay next to me, if that's what she wants. There is a clot of something acid in my throat, and I find it hard to breathe.

In class my pen is constantly slipping and stumbling, throwing small cascades of ink across the page. The soft paw of our language teacher, Valeryi "Three-Lips" Nikolayevitch, descends on my shoulder:

—You have to think, Zarev, think!

How I hate his soft, ingratiating voice. Without having to raise my head I can see his face only too plainly: a pudgy, carelessly modeled face, with a split lower lip. I can see his shiny coat, covered with dandruff, and that flabby hand, with its distended veins under the reddish down . . . . I would like to shrug it off, but all I can do is hang my head even lower. I would like to spit at everything! I try hard not to look at him, for fear of being tempted to throw the inkwell into his ugly mug.

But his voice is purring away above my head, and I can feel myself choking inside that voice, like a fly in a sticky spider's web.

—Oh, oh, Zarev, I can't understand you, honestly . . . . And stand up, if you please, when you're spoken to . . . . Honestly, to call yourself a Young Pioneer . . . .

Suddenly that acid clot in my throat comes retching up. Without looking at anyone I rush up from my seat and out of the classroom.

Warm rain, drizzling on the street. I walk along the low, green-flecked fences, clenching my fists and hating the whole world. The rain is coming stronger now, my face is wet with it, but it has a salty taste. I'm afraid to admit it to myself. After all, I am fourteen now . . . .

I don't feel like going home; home, now, is like the

deserted church by Khytrov pond, full of echoes and emptiness. As long as my father was there, its windows could greet me with warmth and light. Without my father I always felt somehow superfluous, always getting in the way of somebody or something. I was told that I had rickets at birth and used to cry a lot as a baby. And so nobody really liked me—well, that's nothing very unusual. I don't know what my father thought of me, but only he could talk to me as one talks to equals, without putting on a lisp, or trying to force himself upon me. And in return I gave him the only thing I had to give: my devotion.

I hate the whole world. I hate everybody who has the right to bang his fist on the table, to give marks, to order you about with his little whistle at street crossings, or to make you fill in forms . . . . I won't have it! I don't want any part of it! You can all go to hell!

My feet are taking me to the old iron bridge by the old railroad depot. The trains don't stop here, but I've often watched the rumbling freights pass by, picking up speed and disappearing behind the next turn. And in such moments, I am lost to this world . . . .

By the steep shore, in the shade of three ancient palm trees, there is a lonely little hut. The ocean roars against the slope, but the tropical silence above the bamboo roof is guarded by big warm stars in the sky. The hut is lit by an everlasting, melancholy fire. The reflections of its flames lick softly across the walls, across tin plates hanging on the walls, across a face lost in thought: she is waiting. Her name is Taminga. Her father is Eagle Beak, Great Chief of the tribe of the Agu-Oga. Many hunters from neighboring tribes are wooing her, but Taminga is silent, has been silent for almost three years now. And shaken and shattered by her grief, the noble suitors leave her to her grieving.

How sad are the words of her father, the unvanquished Eagle Beak:

—My daughter! For three years you have been silent. The bravest young warriors have come and gone. I am old, the Sun God will soon call me to return to the eternal hunting grounds. And still there is no one to whom I could entrust the fate of my tribe. I implore you, in the name of the star that is shining above our hut, tell me, tell me, daughter, the reason for your grief!

And lovely Taminga replies unto her father:

—Father! I will confess the cause of sadness in my heart. Far, far away, on the other side of this ocean, in a small town with the strange name Yuzhnogorsk, there lives a noble young man, Seryoshka Zarev. But he does not possess a catamaran, he has no craft in which he can cross the ocean, and therefore we are doomed to live our lives in separation, until the day we die. And this is all I have to tell you, my father!

Eagle Beak, the unvanquished, did not reply to his daughter. The Agu-Oga are men of few words. Eagle Beak rises, puts on his moccasins and launches his most seaworthy catamaran. And the lovely Taminga goes down to the shore, looking out to sea for a long time, following her father's journey with her round eyes that have a perennially surprised expression in their depths. And as a sign of her grief she lets her flexible, rubberlike braids fall down on her shoulders.

The shrill whistle of a locomotive returns me to reality. Below, a freight train is floating by. I can see a small man busily making himself comfortable in the brakeman's caboose at the tail end of the train. His head is lost in a huge canvas coat. The train is picking up speed, and the small dark man looks like a silkworm slipping out of its cocoon, vigorously pushing his head out and up into the light. And already the gray mist of distance obscures the red taillight of the train.

I am so full of envy I could burst into tears again. The little man in his canvas coat, sitting there in the brakeman's cabin, looking around, yes, what else is there to do?—just sitting there and looking around . . . . It's warm there, inside the coat. Now I can't even hear the whistle anymore, only a long, quiet sigh, almost a groan. And that train is carried onward by its floating rhythms, up along the ladder of rails to the ends of our gray sky. But perhaps the end of this sky lies right there, beyond the first turning? I'm almost certain it does . . . .

The stale, watery air suddenly makes me feel like retching. That receding whistle strikes an untouched chord, and starts it vibrating, the blood pounding in my ears. And I suddenly find myself running back and forth among the boxcars, playing hide and seek with conductors and controllers; finally I am swallowed up by the somber maw, no, by the hospitable cave of an empty cattle car, smelling of hay, dung, moldering bast mats. Through the curtain of rain the lights of Yuzhnogorsk glitter and fade.

I am soaked to the skin, yet I feel warm and calm. Now I don't have to keep on turning the same thoughts over and over in my head, to the point of disgust: my past life up to this moment seems to have been a dream, and a pretty ridiculous one at that. Faces pass through my mind: the horrified face of my mother; Valeryi Nikolayevitch, his ugly mug; Zina's astonished face; the numb, uncomprehending look on my father's face . . . . I feel a kind of condescending pity toward them all, an adult pity—yes, nothing else, just pity.

The train is gathering speed, and through the moving cloud-gaps I can now see the piercing light of the stars; but it does seem to me that they are warm.

3

⌇⌇⌇⌇⌇⌇⌇⌇⌇⌇⌇⌇⌇⌇⌇⌇⌇⌇⌇⌇⌇⌇⌇⌇⌇⌇⌇⌇⌇⌇⌇⌇⌇⌇⌇⌇⌇⌇

Trapped between the bedsheets I feel like a mouse in a damp tobacco pouch. I must have been sweating streams of water, but my mouth is dry and bitter. The old nurse is sitting beside my bed; a ball of wool has tumbled off the knitting on her knees, dragging a length of yarn under the bed. The blizzard isn't battering against the walls anymore; now it has surrounded the house completely, in a continuous, even howl—like the sound of an oven when it is going at full draft . . . .

—Something to drink, mother!

The old woman starts, clutching at her knitting, the

needles begin a hurried staccato dance, joining one tight little stitch to another.

—I'm thirsty, do you hear me?

Now she really wakes up.

—Yes, yes, just a moment, my little one!

She pronounces that endearment, *"milaï,"* by stretching the last syllable, and this, coming from her mouth, makes it sound surprisingly pleasant. I gulp down the water, greedily, while she is holding the jug to my mouth and repeating in a sing-song voice:

—Drink, my little one, drink, water gives strength, water gives life to all creation . . . .

—Where am I, mother?

—What do you think? You're in Kirilino, in our hospital, where else!

—Is it far from here to Verkhneretchensk?

The old woman takes a towel, wipes the sweat off my forehead.

—My goodness, you get funny ideas. Verkhneretchensk! It's at least a thousand versts to Verkhneretchensk, no less . . . . You have relatives there?

—Yes . . . well, sort of.

Pursing her wrinkled lips in sympathy she mutters:

—That's far away, that is . . . .

I'm immersed in some mental arithmetic: if there weren't any mistakes made, I should now be about halfway to Shatsk. Less than four hundred miles—that wasn't much, for two months of straining across the taiga . . . . That damned fever, always hitting me at the worst of times. Nikolai the Phonograph will be rotting by now, I'm sure of that. To hell with him, he didn't deserve any better. But maybe this is the end of me, too? If only they could save my legs. But if not—well, I'll go anyway. I'll fly at their throats like a wolf if they won't let me, but I'll go. I'd rather have the taiga than . . . .

Steps approaching in the corridor, a woman's steps. I close my eyes. Now I am all ears, and above my head that ghostly whispering begins again.

—Now then?

—He's coming to, he's thawing out. He just woke up for a moment and wanted to know where he was. Seems he is from Verkhneretchensk . . . .

—What can we do, what should we do, Trofimovna? I really don't know. There is no way of getting through to the district capital, and this blizzard is sure to last another three days. But the man, the poor man is near his death. Oh Lord!

—Maybe someone could try to get through with a sled, with the dogs?

—But who would try that? Nobody but witches would ride out in such a purga . . . .

—But he'll die, you'll see, or even worse, he'll lose his legs! And I am sure he has a family, he looks old enough to have a wife and children.

—It's no use crying. We'll just have to wait and see. It's three days, too, since Varvara started . . . .

—And it won't come?

—She's a strong woman, but it's a long time . . . .

—But that's nothing serious, anyway. If the child were a small one, it would pop out, just like that: but it's probably more like its father!

—Its father, yes . . . . He spends almost all night in front of her door.

—Well, there'll be another overnight guest soon.

—Who do you mean?

—Our young Nikolay, who else?

—But, they haven't been to the registry office . . . .

—Well, that's the new fashion.

—My God, these young people . . . .

These quiet words, even if a bit sentimental, make me suddenly aware of lives that are utterly alien to me, almost incomprehensible.

4

~~~~~~

I don't like dancing. What's more, I hate it. And I have my reasons: it keeps me from my sleep. Every night, from seven o'clock to one in the morning, these couples are shuffling across the floor, the brass blaring away above me, rattling, booming, and howling tunes fit to drive you out of your mind. I turn and toss in my little cave beneath the dance floor, unable to get some sleep. Damn the first man who ever started jumping about to these rhythms! I want to sleep, my god, I want to sleep. Why can't they lay off it, tell me, what sort of pleasure is there anyway in clutching and dragging each other across a floor like that? But then, suddenly, sleep comes tumbling down, crushing and choking me . . . . And as soon as the first rays of the morning sun strike through the narrow cracks in my low ceiling I wake, to crawl out and run down to the beach.

The sea lies in front of me like an enormous monster, yet a good-humored and, it seems, weightless one; and like a tiny, peaceful animal I now sleep through the morning, to the tune of the murmuring lullabies sung by that light green water. My dreams have wings, they're wheeling and flying, very different from the ones I have at night.

Then I go down to the railroad depot. Waving a rope above my head I run the length of the seven o'clock train from Tiflis:

—Who needs a worker? Who needs a worker?

An hour later, at eight o'clock sharp, I stand by the door of the pastry cook Dadiko Shomiya. He is a morose Mingrelian, with a clean-shaven head and a fat, hairy chest showing through the unbuttoned jacket.

I help him carry his little tables to three schools nearby. At noon I take these same tables to the beach, and later in the evening I transport them to the park. For this, Shomiya gives me three rubles and a certain amount of security, by claiming that I'm a distant relation of his. It's a good thing I am almost blackened by the sun and know the Georgian lingo pretty well, by now . . . .

In between times I go to the market place to see what I can pick up. I've got a little harpoon-stick hidden away in a drainpipe; with this in my hand I stroll past the fruit

stalls, and for those who don't know, I'm just a kid playing with a stick, nothing strange about that. But as soon
as one of the shopkeepers turns or bends behind his stall,
my stick strikes like a falcon, to provide me with my
chosen prey—an apple, a tomato, a slice of meat. Then,
in a quiet corner of the market, I peddle my takings to
the small and faded old women, almost a hundred years
old, who are willing to spend their pension money on
these things. By the end of the day I've made a cher-
vonets,* sometimes even more. Yet I'm not such an old
hand at this mercenary life; it's about eighteen months
now since I last saw the lights of Yuzhnogorsk disappear
behind the railroad embankment. But among the local
crowd of hoodlums I enjoy a certain prestige; they've
noticed how steadily I am making it without ever getting copped. Well, I know myself that I'm way ahead of
them, but I am careful not to show this, as they might
start knocking me around for my snottiness . . . .

My life is very well-organized and regular, inter-
rupted only by short, violent attacks of malarial fever,
which started during the first months of my life here in
the South. When this happens, I usually get weak-
kneed around noon, feel shivery and worn out, and I
know what to do: I go to the beach, bed down in a
trough of hot pebbles and rocks and stay there as long
as the crisis lasts, shivering and shaking with the fever.
The pebbles just burn my skin, without warming or
calming me. After about two hours the attack is over.

---

* Ten ruble note.

Only a dull ache in every muscle of my body reminds me of it, until nightfall.

At night I make my way to the hideout, with great cunning and care, avoiding all lights of the town, and there, below the open-air dance floor, shielded from the world by its planks and boards, I feel like a sovereign prince. I am my own master, my own chief in everything.

And my dreams are always the same: a steep ocean shore, crowned with three palm trees. If only they'd stop that brassy honking above my head! Yeah, I don't like those dancers. What's more, I hate them . . . .

5

~~~~~~

The blizzard is still raging and blowing hard against
the ice flowers on the panes of the net-curtained window. I feel mortally petrified in my dressings. Nothing
but a small part of me is still alive—my brain. There is
no one by my side just now, but the door leading to the
corridor is wide open, and voices talking at the end of
the corridor reach my ears. One of them has already become familiar—a thin, singing kind of voice; the other
I now hear for the first time. It sounds like a rough,
cracking, young man's voice.

And the first voice is saying:

—You've told me these things a hundred times. But

yesterday you stayed in the reading room again, with her, long into the night, and then you even walked her home! Don't tell me it isn't true.

And the other one:

—But you're crazy, Galka! That's part of my duties —the Skolkova girl has only just joined us, she doesn't know anybody yet, and she's a city girl, too. If we don't take a little care of her, she'll lose interest and chuck everything! And it's true that she is different, from out of town . . . .

—Just you go on taking care of everybody, and I'll certainly be out of this town—pretty soon!

—But I'm telling you, let's get married!

—Should I feel honored? Is that the way to make a proposal? Just like that—come on, let's go and get married! Oh, Kolya!

—And why not? Why should we worry about frills and formalities? We live in fast and hard times, so lets get it over and done with—we'll get married tomorrow.

—But of course, I'm all yours, for the asking—what a hero!

—Oh why can't you stop that . . . How is he, anyway?

—If Ivan Antonovitch doesn't get here, he'll die. It's an inflammation. We give him sedatives; without them he'd be howling with pain, all the time . . . .

—So he's going to die—after I dragged him here, and all that trouble . . . . Well there you are, brother Nikolai, son of Pyotr: a village crammed with people, and we just look on, while a man is dying!

I feel amused by the talk of this yellow-beaked young ostrich: concealing his egotism behind great humanitarian airs. He won't go himself, oh no, he'll just "organize" things and hang around to pinch this girl's sweet little buttocks. If you only knew, my boy, if you'd only known who it was you were saving, you would have made a detour of forty versts to avoid finding me!

Out of the corner of my eye I glance into the corridor: there he stands, leaning his shoulder against the wall. A tall boy, with a wild shock of hair, but a weak-chinned face. He's toying with the belt of his jacket, carelessly thrown over his shoulders.

—I'll go and talk to the boys. If they're afraid, I'll go alone!

That does the trick—how her voice changes! Nothing left of that studied indifference. And without seeing her I know she is trembling all over, down to the tiniest little nerve-end.

—But Kostyenka, for God's sake, you can't do that! No one can drive across the taiga in a blizzard like this!

—Come on, you can't say that—think of him! He's dying, don't you understand?

It is obvious that he's trying to convince himself just as much as the girl. I listen, avidly. How is it going to end, anyway? I'm not afraid of dying, not at all. What frightens me is the possibility of losing my legs, as the old woman said; death does not worry me. I guess I'm a rather primitive type of being. In the labor camp our inveterate novel reader Ziama, who had swallowed more than his share of books, explained to me how only the most primitive organisms do not know fear, are not afraid of dying, and how they're able to survive for this very reason even in the most incredible circumstances. And it is true—I've kept going where many others died; in the South, or as a prisoner of war. But to lose your legs! I'm no earthworm, I can't go on living if I'm cut in two like that. If one really wanted to classify me among the different species of primitive organisms, I suppose only the millipede fits the description: I must be able to run.

The conversation in the corridor is quieter now, almost incomprehensible.

He:

—Do you understand?

She:

—Yes . . . . Yes, I do.

He:

—We have to do it, Galya.

She:

—Yes, Kolya, we have to do it.

He:

—There's no one else who could even try . . . .

She:

—No, there is no one else, Kolya . . . .

Like an echo, repeating itself in the mountains, lulling me to sleep. But damn it, the last thing shooting through my mind is a sense of resentment: against whom? And why?

6

~~~~~~

Until now I've always recognized my little cave by its habitual smell of rotting leaves, old rags and moldering planks. But today I've lost my sense of smell completely —I've been unloading cement at the depot with a couple of other bums, for some smart-guy businessman, and my nose is clogged up with that sticky dust. It's hellish hard work, too. Two of us climbing into a car, throwing exactly fifty shovelfuls of the stuff outside, no more, no less, then rushing out again ourselves, back into the fresh air, and then again into another car . . . . We're half dead by the time evening comes, but each of us has made a fortune: thirty rubles per head! And then we get all the grub we want, on the boss. It's past midnight when we leave, all the others rushing off to buy some drink, but me shuffling on home, pleased as all hell. I've never made this much in a day.

They've finished with their damn dancing, hours ago. I grope about in the darkness to find the two secret boards, and having found and replaced them above myself I suddenly notice there's someone already there! And this someone says, in a murmuring, drunken, sleepy voice:

—Come on, you won't be sorry . . . .

Furious little hammers start throbbing in my temples. I've never had a woman yet; there was the little girl with pigtails, and all I did was carry her satchel and share an apple with her during recess . . . . And after that, there was only the wistful dream of the three ancient palm trees. The other kids, making it in ways similar to my own, often bragged about their sex adventures in great detail; and I'd often seen the wild orphan girls, especially the older ones, disappear into the dark shadows by the Rioni river, followed by some of these hoodlums. But what did I care for them? I just wasn't interested.

Now she is yawning, a long, voluptuous yawn, blowing a reek of stale vodka into my dulled nostrils.

—So what's wrong, hey? I'm not good enough for you, or something?

A pair of clammy hands start moving over my body in the dark, touching me, begging me to give it to her . . . . I push them away, choking: but a great feeling of power comes surging up into my mind, and then,

I'm drunk with it, my head is reeling with this warmth, and it is uttering almost senseless words through my mouth—terrible words like the wind soughing through a forest at night, yet others as vague and tender as morning mist rising out of the sea.

She wakes me up in the morning. Avoiding her eyes I affect a gloomy mumble:

—What's it to be now?

She laughs, derisively.

—Don't you try to kid me! It was your first time, wasn't it? I'm sure it was. I can tell . . . .

—Oh, shut up!

—Now who do you think you are? You could at least say thank you—I only did it because I was stoned out of my mind, anyway . . . .

She looks about fifteen, maybe sixteen. But the first wrinkles have already begun their outward journey from the corners of her eyes, and those eyes—large, gray, very much like two round pebbles on the beach— are lit from within, with a good, clear light, looking almost improbable in that small, pinched, gray-skinned face. And it seems to me I recognize something in those eyes: perhaps my childhood?

She starts combing her hair, and a thin ray of sunlight, coming through a narrow crack between the floorboards, moves across her raised arm, illuminating the pale skin close to the elbow. I can see all the little veins underneath. An unknown feeling of gratitude makes me say:

—And why are you one of those . . . ?

Again, the same ironical tone:

—Never mind that—you'll get used to it. What's it mean, anyway? But it would be great to have a drink now, to chase that early morning itch . . . d'you have anything to eat?

Using a rag for a napkin I get up a breakfast of a couple of corn cakes, tomatoes, salt.

—And now you'll go and get drunk again.

—Well, dogs howl when they're feeling low, but I'm a human being, I think . . . .

—Why don't you go to one of those colonies for orphaned girls?

—I've been in one . . . .

—Come on, I don't believe you!

The girl raises her dirty little fist in a threatening gesture. I keep looking at her. I offer her an apple, and again something faraway, something old and secret flashes through my mind. With pointed squirrel teeth she bites into the apple, folds her legs so that her knees are touching my shoulder and starts talking, in a lively, excited, jerky sort of way:

—Listen now. I met this guy yesterday, I think he's some kind of a thief, but a smart one, you know, and tough. His name is Albert Ivanovitch. And when we'd finished our business, he makes this other proposal. He says he needs a couple of slim kids who are fast on their feet. I guess he's a housebreaker or something. This is what he says: "Two or three kids, that's what I need." And the first one I thought of was you! I've known you a long time, you see. And I've been wise to your hide-

out, too. You see I noticed you last spring, you're a
lone wolf, you never steal anything, you want to make
it all alone . . . . And I like going down to the beach in
the early mornings, too . . . . Anyway, this man Albert
Ivanovitch gives me his address and says to come and
see him when it gets dark. You'll come with me, won't
you? I'll have a try at this burglary racket, at least I
don't have to let everybody jump me, that way. Now,
what do you say?

—I'm not playing that game. No, I have all I want.

—And what are you going to do when winter comes?

—What winter? There's no real winter, here. I'll
spend the winter in my cave, right here—it's going to
be better anyway, no more dances, no cops, peace and
quiet . . . .

—But it's hard to make any money in winter! If you
don't want to go along with me, I don't care. I just want
to be with somebody who is good to me . . . .

—My god, you're a crazy one. What could I be to
you?

She smiles.

—You're close to me now.

—But, no. I can't get mixed up in anything like that.

A look of almost doglike longing comes into her eyes.

—But maybe he isn't a thief at all! Who knows what
it's about? And he said, I'll get you clothes, I'll get you
some shoes . . . . And he said, eat, drink! And he promised to get us a place to stay . . . .

Reluctantly, I give in.

—All right. We'll go and see.

Now she is radiant, so tremendously pleased that I suddenly realize—a great shock—how bruised and humiliated she must be. In the morning light the town is checkered with broad, bold stripes of light and shade. Looking across the rooftops there's the sea, breathing like a great beast. There aren't many people about yet, in the streets. We walk along the deserted beach and lie down on the still cold pebbles; above our heads a herd of weightless clouds floats across a benevolent sky. I fix my gaze on the sun-drenched horizon, but I can't see the steep shores, the three palm trees, I can't even see the melancholy face anymore, frozen in its endless vigil. All tales must end, somewhere.

7

~~~~~~

How long have I slept? An hour, a year? My legs ache. It's as if they had been soaked in ice water. The girl with the high cheekbones is on duty; she is staring hard, through the window. What does she see out there? What is she thinking about? Feeling my eyes on her, she shudders, turns around. A kind of smile passes over her puffy lips:

—We're holding up all right?

It is obvious that she is asking the question out of habit. She is standing near the window, completely in darkness. I have no time to play at pretty phrases. I ask her as brusquely as I can, so she doesn't have time to pity me:

—Nurse, are they going to cut my legs off?

She shudders once again and is silent for a moment, as if still thinking over what the question meant. Then she begins to speak, quickly, convincingly:

—Of course not, dear comrade—of course not, why should they? Everything will be all right, everything, everything! In the morning they'll bring back Ivan Antonovitch—they'll certainly bring him back—and everything will be just fine.

But I feel, feel physically, in all my guts, that at this moment she doesn't want to convince *me*, but someone else: someone there, on the other side of the window, on the taiga. I get even with her in my own way:

—All you do is lie, nurse!

That gets her. In her surprise, she drops the thermometer she had been preparing for me. She starts. Her pointed chin quivers, and now there are fast, troubled tears running down her tanned cheeks. With her head lowered, she almost runs to the door. All I can hear is the crunch of the thermometer glass breaking under the soles of her sandals.

Sima comes in a minute later. In the past, I used to know her only by her voice and her way of walking; now I see her face at last. Sima is strong; she is a woman over thirty, with narrow, slit eyes in a puffy face . . . . She really seemed much more attractive from her voice. I wait for her rebuke with the calm of a man who doesn't care. But she plants herself on the stool and starts telling me what's going on, in a confidential sort of way:

—You must forgive her, my dear friend. She's still young, she has no experience, and besides she's very upset. Her fiancé has gone to the district capital, with the dogs, to bring back our doctor Ivan Antonovitch. Over here, you never travel in a blizzard like this, and she being in her fourth month, yes . . . . So, don't judge her badly! And now here's a little sleeping pill for you, my dear friend—there we are, like that . . . . I have to leave you now, I don't feel too well today, heart trouble . . . . This kind of weather, you know . . . .

Sima goes out heavily on her swollen legs. The girl with the cheekbones tiptoes in to take her place once again. She thinks I'm already asleep, sits down silently beside the bed. Through my half-closed eyelids I again notice that her eyes move toward the same spot—beyond the window. It's as if her whole being is flying out through the darkness and the snow, to him . . . . Come on, you, dumb little creature with cheekbones, why did I come to make you suffer? To hell with me!

8

Albert Ivanovitch has a strange face: sharp features, chalky skin, full of reddish whiskers, down and around his chin . . . . It's hard to say exactly how old Albert Ivanovitch is. Sometimes you might give him forty years, sometimes sixty. When he smiles, when he laughs, or even when he bursts out laughing, it seems that only the muscles of his face are moving—but that he himself, his body, his eyes, are tensed like a cat about to spring.

In the dark, I can't make out Albert Ivanovitch; but I still feel his eyes upon me, nailing me to the spot. It's disgusting—I never before thought that a man could have such power over another. It's like a nightmare: something horrible catching you, and you no longer have the force to move hand or foot. But when you sleep, you wake up. But this agony—it's been three years I haven't been able to get out of it. For three years now his stare nails me to the spot as soon as I think of running away.

The only question I dared to ask him on the day we met has remained my first and last . . . . In response, Albert Ivanovitch just laughed and said in his sneering, affected way:

—Who I am? You're a funny guy! I am a sahr-cus pah-formah . . . . You've been to the sahr-cus? Well, that's it. I'm a magician . . . . Just like a magician, I can make anything a sick soul wants appeah, out of an empty tophat—from a rabbit to silk stockings. So, my friend, you can call yourself lucky indeed, and your la-dy twice as lucky.

Since that time, I don't ask anything, I just listen. Everything—his way of talking carelessly and mockingly, his way of dressing, even that affected, faintly military accent—everything sets Albert Ivanovitch apart from the men I used to deal with. He looks people straight in the eye, without blinking, as if to nail them to the wall. Some of them don't realize it, but I for my part know that with his indifferent eyes my master sees, grasps and remembers many things. Otherwise he couldn't live. Albert Ivanovitch is a smuggler, the last of the Mohicans, as he calls himself.

I make up for my feeling of powerlessness before my boss by a hidden hatred. And I'm keeping books. I really hope Albert Ivanovitch will settle, one fine day. My accounts begin with Valka; that great night has not left my memory. I see Valka always the way I saw her that morning, scornful, provoking. But Albert Ivanovitch intends her to stay with him. And that's the *law*. And it may seem that I've given in: but I'm not forgetting a thing. All I have to do is remember that night, and I'm flooded with wild anger. In those moments I'm ready to kill him. But let me meet his glance and in an instant I withdraw, I am quenched.

It's three years now that I've been crossing the border. I don't know what I carry, it's none of my business. That's for the boss to know, he's the one who holds all the cards. It's dangerous to cross the border, but it's not very difficult. The border village is divided in half—one part is ours, the other is the Turks'. During the day, relatives can visit each other simply by using a pass good for one time. But the night does not put an end to family feeling . . . .

Albert Ivanovitch does not cross the border. I'm the one who does. In case of bad luck I'd only get the labor camp, he would get death. But you see, that doesn't worry the boss too much. I'm the third to work for Albert Ivanovitch. In a moment of drunken sincerity, he slaps me on the shoulder in his condescending way:

—Sery-osha, you're a lucky fellow. You're lasting long-ah than any of the others. It's cleah that you're a lucky man. And anyway, I've really gotten used to you. You know how to listen, and that's the merit of a wise man. If you only last until my day comes . . . .

Today the "day" has come. That is why we are sitting

facing each other in a cellar near the border. For three years now this house has served us as a hideout. Its owner, a swindler from Batum named Sandro, is organizing the last crossing for us tonight. We're leaving forever, never to return. Beyond the border. We are sitting down, and we are silent. We have nothing to say. We're going. Forever, never to return.

Three years is a long time, especially for me. But during this time, I was not able to guess who my boss was: who was he, why was he doing this? The mystery is simply beyond me. As at the time of our first meeting, Albert Ivanovitch frightens me and attracts me, like an abandoned house.

I rarely see him happy and talkative. In general, he only talks when drunk, and then he talks at length and incomprehensibly:

—In the system of the world, what are we? A bluff, a mirah-ge! Is it not conceivable that what we mortals call the system of the world is only a molecule of shit, dropped by an insect living in an inconceivable world? . . . And suddenly, theah it is, falling on your head! The revolution! Heah's to you! Why, what fo-ah? As far as I'm concerned, I would not be any the less an independent planet, I would still be my own universe, certainly my own government . . . . So get the hell out of here, you ungrateful cattle! At first, they stand and shuffle on the doorstep: "You wouldn't want to give us a little bread for the winter?" And then, they go and crap into the *historical* vah-ses of the Winter Palace! I can understand a revolution with Robespierre, La Conciergerie, the nights of the Convention! Now hea-ah, what do we have? Vaska and Trishka, Prov and Nikishka .... The hell!

And then, carried away on a wave of drunkenness, he lets loose.

—Let me tell you, old boy, life can only be made good through danger, risk, wild flights, the nevah-ending drunken binge of a Cossack! Life in itself is just rottenness—that's why you have to burn your candle at both ends, and not glow out gently. Whereas prison, m'boy, is an intermission—nothing but an intermission between the acts, a little walk to the buffet .... You, for exahmple, do you know what the Imperial Guard means? Anyway, how could you have learned, since all your ancestors were cattle, from generation to generation? Thank God at least *you'll* become a man. But as for the others, let them go to the devil, all of them! Valka, take off your clothes! Drink, we live but once!

Now we are sitting down, and we are silent. We keep sitting and we continue to be quiet. Soon we'll have to go out. I am afraid, as if I had the cramps in the middle of a lake. Anxiety is hollowing me out in a disgusting way. Without glass after glass of wine served me by Albert Ivanovitch, I'd surely whine like a puppy. My hands are shaking, the wine spills out of the glass. My drunkenness is not blotting out the present, it is only filling my head with a cast-iron weight. I have probably gone and come back a hundred times, but today there is no coming back. And this strikes me dumb. Once again, as in my childhood, I have the feeling of being a tiny, negligible grain of sand lost in the vast foreign world. Where will I land? Why? In chaos, thoughts, memories, presentiments are knotting in my mind, and there is a bitter clot in my throat.

At the other end of the table, a match is struck. In the darkness, a small tongue of flame outlines the face of Albert Ivanovitch. As he lights his cigarette he looks at me through the flame. I know he has a habit of letting the match burn down to the end by holding it by the part just burned. This time, he puts out the match while it is only half burned. Before it goes out, I notice that his fingers are trembling. But it is possible that I am deluding myself. Now the red eye of the cigarette is covered with ashes, now it revives, as if it wanted to light up my thoughts in the darkness.

—Have a cigarette!

—Don't feel like it.

—That will pass.

—I don't feel too good.

—You're scared?

—I told you, I don't feel good.

—I know, that happens. The first time, it's always like that.

—But will there be a second time?

—That depends on you.

—I don't understand.

—You'll understand later.

—When?

—On the other side.

—What are we going to do in a foreign country?

—Money, my friend, is the best passport and the best language. As long as you're with me, you'll have nothing to worry about.

Already I no longer sense the abrupt, demanding intonations in Albert Ivanovitch's voice. I grow bolder:

—But what am I going to do for you, Albert Ivanovitch?

The eye of the cigarette glows angrily, but goes out again.

—You wouldn't understand, old boy. But the main ideah is more or less this: in a foreign country, an old pirate likes to have a piece of familiar living flesh with him . . . . It's sentimental—but there will also be business . . . .

This was the point at which our relations would break off. If the old wolf could have guessed what a mistake he had just made! As long as I felt myself held on a leash by his stare, he could rest easy; I didn't have the courage to rebel. But now that a passing weakness had made him stumble in the dark, Albert Ivanovitch, the all-powerful Albert Ivanovitch, did not even notice how he had fallen . . . .

But I am not in a hurry. I wait for my moment. I listen. To listen is the dignity of the wise. It appears that that's what Albert Ivanovitch teaches.

I hear light footsteps. Now someone cautiously opens the door, revealing a patch of starless sky. The darkness begins to whisper, in Valka's voice:

—Sandro said that we could go ahead.

—Softer, you silly bitch! And close the door.

I feel I am getting more and more sober every minute. I know, I know with certainty that at this moment Valka, hidden in the dark, is not looking my way but is staring at the reddening eye of the cigarette, is looking at it as she had looked at me—with the eyes of a devoted dog, shining eyes. This infuriates me; I feel that my anger is going to explode like a wad of guncotton.

The little glow, after reddening one last time, is crushed out in a mess of sparks on the table.

—God be with us.

Valka and I take the load on our backs. To believe Albert Ivanovitch, it's the last load. For his part, Albert Ivanovitch goes out with his hands free, by way of precaution, as he says. We go out Indian file into the stifling August night. Albert Ivanovitch at the head, behind him Valka, behind Valka, myself. I still haven't decided on anything definite, but I already know that I will not go beyond those mountains that stand up like huge chunks of blackness before my eyes. There is nothing for me there, nothing. I cannot accept the "forever." To be deprived forever of the earth that I am bound to by every drop of my blood. To lose forever the hope of finding the kind of people I am searching for. Can a man abandon his last hope?

The silhouette of Sandro suddenly appears before us on the path. He tells us:

—They have passed. The next patrol won't be around for another half hour. You will have time, *batono*.

And he disappears as if he had never existed. We keep

on walking. The little river flows evenly, without splashing. The stones, polished by the water, slide under our feet as if they were soaped. We advance, following Albert Ivanovitch's advice, without raising our feet, but sliding them along as if on skis; this doesn't make less noise, it's only harder to walk. The water swirls around our ankles and it seems that it doesn't simply murmur, but that it makes an uproar to wake up the surrounding region.

When at last the bottoms of my feet feel the first dry stone, I hear the voice of Albert Ivanovitch:

—Thank God, we're through!

And I can't believe my ears: he has lost his arrogant tone on the way . . . .

He says to me:

—Go ahead, I'll catch up with you.

I walk in silence, in the night. But at the end of ten steps, I stop. My hearing is as sensitive as an unhealed wound. Something heavy has just fallen on the pebbles of the bank. I guess it. One of our sacks. Then a metallic noise comes to me. Albert Ivanovitch operating the safety catch of his gun. And:

—About face!

—What d'you mean, Albert Ivanovitch! You promised . . . .

—Turn around, you whore!

Valka does not speak, she whines:

—Albert Ivanovitch, Albert Ivanovitch . . . . Why? Why? When I've done everything for you . . . .

—Come on, you bitch, I don't have time . . . .

And not the slightest trace of that guardsman's accent!

—They won't even put me in the camp, now that I'm an adult. I'll be back on the streets, Albert Ivanovitch!

She screams. At that very moment, my decision is made. I begin to act automatically, like a sleepwalker. I grope for a chunk of stone under my feet. I rip it out of the cold ground. I wave it over my head. Like this, I run over the ten steps that separate me from Albert Ivanovitch. The noise of the river deadens my footsteps. I can clearly see the two silhouettes. She is on her knees in the water. He is standing with his leg raised to kick her.

Our blows are struck almost at the same time. He falls and crushes Valka with his whole weight. She splashes around in the water, getting free. Probably she still doesn't understand anything. I make a motion toward her, but Valka throws herself aside, out of my reach, and grabs a stone:

—Bastard! Oh you bastard! You attacked him from behind! Oh you bastard! Don't come near me!

Her face turned toward me, she backs off step by step into the dark, repeating:

—Bastard! He picked you up from the gutter and you . . . . Oh you bastard!

What did I want from Valka when I brandished my stone over the master's head? Gratitude, repentance, submission? It is possible that it wasn't any one of those. She screamed, and her scream, like a spark, set off an explosion of the rage accumulated in me for three years.

She yells: you bastard! Yes, of course. Bastard. All at
once I'm filled with a terrible indifference. The darkness is still whispering something, but I no longer listen.
I go back into the water and move forward without
thought or aim. I don't care where I go. I'm sick of
everything. But above all, I'm sick of looking out for
myself . . . .

—Halt! Who goes there?

A little soldier with a rifle appears before me. He has
a flat nose and he is very, very young. It is daylight
now, and I see clearly. I even see a hard glint in his
eyes—probably because of the bayonet. He is nineteen.
And how much older am I? A hundred years, at least?
If not more. If not more . . . .

—Put up your hands!

I obediently raise my hands.

9

Incredible, to realize the skill hidden in Sima's flabby hands and body—but it is no accident that those hands are like those of a doll; any pickpocket would gladly give half his living life to have such hands . . . . What use has a pickpocket for the other half of his life, anyway? But even yesterday the time of wound-dressing had seemed like an hour of torture on the rack. I could not bear the slightest, lightest touch; but now Sima's hands are working wonders on me. I force myself not to look in her direction, for fear of seeing my own legs . . . . They must be black by now, I think; some time passes, and I still don't feel any pain at all, only the balm-drenched dressing, slowly winding off my skin, reminds me that the session is in full swing . . . .

While working her magic Sima keeps talking, repeating herself:

—Now we're going to fix you up properly, you good soul you. Five minutes, that's all we need. A mite of ichthyol to revive you, and to dope your legs a little, and then we'll hit Old Devil Pain with a shot of penicillin, too. And the pain will be gone, gone—now isn't that something? Now you just hold it, my little one, just hold it a tiny little while—and now you be a big strong man, a real hero; and I don't even know your first name?

—Sergei.

—Oh! Silovna—she says to the old woman assisting her—what a wonderful patient we have here, he is worth his weight in gold, and that is God's truth! Here I am, tormenting him with my clumsy paws, and he takes it, he can take it all . . . . Now, Silovna, hold the bandage—yes, that's it. And now the right leg . . . . One more minute of agony, Seryoshenka! That's it. There we are, Silovna. Now this, and that, and that . . . . All over now. Poo-oof!

She wipes the beads of sweat off her forehead with the back of her hand, honest pride shining from her eyes:

—Those aren't just any old pair of legs, now, they are masterpieces well worth admiring! They're pretty hot now, pain always gives off heat, God yes, how it gives off heat . . . . Cover him up, Silovna.

It is true: the pain is receding, as if obeying her incantations. But Sima does not calm down yet:

—I haven't told you the latest news, have I? Of course I haven't. The communications are working again, and Ivan Antonovitch is on his way! Ivan Antonovitch is coming to raise one man from the dead . . . . And now we have to eat, and then eat some more. You can't just lie there forever, without any nourishment at all!

I try to resist. The word "nourishment" makes my guts churn over in rebellion. But Sima won't stop waving her hands like a mother-hen flapping her wings:

—You're going to be the end of me, Seryosha! What will Ivan Antonovitch say? I'm sorry, but this really is a scandal, your not eating a single bite for two days on end! One has to eat, one way or another, my little one, one way or another . . . . I'll make you something right away, and you'll like it.

She shuffles out, and the old woman follows her. I am alone. The windows appear coated over with dense, blue paint; it's the dawn, now filling the room with light-rays resembling watery ripples and reflections. The wind that has been tearing through the house has now become intermittent, pausing more frequently and for longer periods, as if the blizzard had run out of breath. But at each new onslaught the curtains in front of the window tremble, and the big guns of thunder are still hammering away without interruption, in the dark center of this tempest.

This Sima! Yes, she has indeed touched me on my

most sensitive point . . . . Where to find refuge now, against myself? For twenty years I've suffocated my memories in drink, in hatred, in convulsions of fighting for a place in the sun. But what can I do now, left alone with the memories closing in on me, dissolving me like a lump of tin ore in an acid bath . . . . This is the second time in my life that I have met a human being who accidentally or, perhaps, intentionally exposes my soul to the divine light, and makes it writhe in pain like a snail torn out of its shell.

Old Silovna enters, solemnly bearing a bowl of steaming soup as if it were the champion's cup in some athletic contest. The wrinkles around her eyes are like little accordions: she's smiling triumphally, exhibiting her remaining two teeth.

—You try this soup of ours—no one ever made soup like this at Verkhneretchensk! They couldn't possibly . . . . You'll see, you'll wolf it down. It's sterlet soup!

She starts spoonfeeding me, and I swallow the hot and oily broth without sensing smell or taste. But I feel slowly engulfed by a burning, wearying warmth, I cannot resist any longer. While she is feeding me the old woman goes on talking:

—There we go, little one, now eat your fill, and it's true, isn't it, that they don't make anything like it at home, at Verkhneretchensk? It is true they don't know how to make this soup, do they now?

This time, I don't have to lie. I try to reply in the same vein.

—No, they don't make anything like it.

—Simotchka has really devoted herself to you, that's the way she is, she is so generous, and always doing so much good. But what's in it for her? Nothing at all, nothing, nothing at all . . . .

—Yes, well it's true, it's wonderful . . . .

—Now now, my dear boy, "wonderful," yes wonderful indeed, but you don't know her, you don't know our Sima. She doesn't have a doctor's certificate, but she's just as good as any doctor! Ivan Antonovitch brought us back here, from the front, and how she took care of the men down there! Everything she does, she does it more with her heart than with her hands. She has given all her strength, all that heart to others, so that she herself is hardly more than a sigh. And just imagine, she had a little rest by the stove, and she had to take to her bed—it just didn't suit her, to stay by the stove! But of course, that isn't her way at all, she has to do everything herself, just by herself, all alone. Yes yes, one might say that the three schools nearby, all the children in them are Sima's godchildren, it's she who brought them all into this world . . . .

Suddenly I feel I have to put on my protective mental armor: enough of this stupid sentimentality! It is just that these people do not know me. If ever they get to know the truth, they will abandon me without hesitation, they'll be too disgusted to crush me. Now I have to play along with them, play the game of "loser takes all." Just to keep my legs; and he with the fewest illusions is always the winner. That's it, isn't it, Ziama? In this game I could give them a handicap of a hundred points; but as soon as I feel the ground under my feet again, I won't care less, a dozen of these people are nothing to me. I have to get to Shatsk. To the floorboards, the hiding place, the place of rest . . . .

Food and warmth take effect on me. I feel drowsy. I close my eyes. The thin film that separates dreams from reality, thin like a razor's edge, now sticks in my throat in the shape of a question I had long forgotten: "You accuse men; but have you really been living among men?"

I cry out, inside myself, a wild and frantic yell to drown these noises of my soul: "Don't you try to indoctrinate me, Semyon Semyonovitch, cut that propaganda out, I'm telling you to cut it out! My blood is freezing as it is . . . ."

And the old woman, still whispering, whispering:

—Oh, yes, yes yes . . . .

10

~~~~~~

We are marching westward, or, in fact, we are being herded toward the west like cattle. We: that is, a long column of prisoners of war. We're marching in stages, from one camp to another, and every time we start out again there aren't quite as many left in the column. What is the goal of this endless trek? The Lord alone knows. Or probably even He doesn't know. If he does, why doesn't He put an end to it, anyway? We are marching in ranks, six abreast, and these little groups of six try to stick together. Wherever changes or new groupings occur, this is only due to the customary losses . . . . It is easy to see that the force of habit, of striving for some kind of community, which is akin to the instinct for self-preservation, works in the minds of men until the very last instant of their lives.

Our luck is none too good. The losses are great. But those who are left stick to their little groups with great perseverance. To be exact, there are only three left, of this sturdy breed: myself, my neighbor Semyon Semyonovitch, and Uncle Vanya, who invariably walks third in. Uncle Vanya has eye trouble: his heavily swollen eyelids remain half-shut, resembling the eyes of a sleeping hen. To be able to see anything at all he has to raise his chin, and this gives him an arrogant air, especially when seen in profile. But Uncle Vanya is a good guy, and a timid one at that. During the overnight halts and the rest pauses on the march he lies flat on his back on the ground, his face turned up to the sky, his hands stretched out by his sides, touching his trouser seams, and thus he remains, immobile, until the signal is given for departure. Uncle Vanya marches in complete silence, and with such a careful and measured step that it seems almost grotesque; you'd think he is afraid of spilling over, like the water from a brimming flower vase. It seems to me that inside him there is some tremendous charge, which no one has yet invented the proper words to express.

Semyon Semyonovitch marches on the extreme right. He is a small, slightly built man, all veins and tendons. He's a furrier from Moscow. I don't know how he keeps going, with his open belly-wound, covered with a bandage improvised from a shirt-rag. But day and night he is scheming escape; all the while on the march he keeps gnawing his thumb, calculating, evaluating and measuring some unknown thing. He's a real eccentric, if you ask me. What's the use of escape! Let them fight, let them fly at each other's throats—as far as I'm concerned I won't lift a finger for this racket. It's not for nothing that I've been in the clink three times: let them all go to hell! But nevertheless Semyon Semyonovitch and his passionate tenacity do inspire involuntary admiration.

We met back in Lozovaïa, as we were unloaded from the boxcars. The liquidations began as soon as we were out of town, in a provisional camp—which was just a barbed wire enclosure on an old kolkhoz. The Jews and the political commissars were picked out and shot right away, about three hundred yards from the camp, and thrown into the abandoned entrenchments. It does seem frightening to start with, but as time wears on, you get used to it; soon no one pays any attention to shots or screams. You have to look out for yourself, that is the rational thing to do. The first volunteer informers begin to appear. They watch out for "undesirables" and sometimes bully the prisoners. There is a particularly zealous one, a small, mean stoolie with a broken nose, smashed as if by a blow. Like a rat he keeps scuttling back and forth among the prisoners lying stretched out on the ground for a rest. He picks on soldiers who are lying face down:

—Now why is that guy hiding his *nose*, hey? You a Jew or something? Or a commissar, maybe? You bastard . . . .

I see how he finally pounces on his prey, after many false starts and fruitless efforts—almost squealing with pleasure:

—Now I got you, didn'I, got you and your ugly commissar's mug, didn'I? What you done with it? What you done with Russia? Sold her, that's what, you've sold her all right!

Like a top he spins around a huge, red-haired horse of a prisoner, who is wearing a sky-blue, torn sweater. The man does not say anything, just stands there resting his chin on his collarbone, his back against the wall of a barn. There is so much weariness and desperate indifference in his stooped figure that it seems he wouldn't start to budge even if the sky came tumbling down . . . .

The small man keeps jumping up and down in front of him, shoving his dirty, shriveled fist into his face, then turning back to the other prisoners as if to get their acclaim:

—Hey brothers, this is the big chief, isn't it? I obeyed him, didn'I? And he's sucked my blood, he has . . . . You've sold her, haven't you, you've sold old Russia?

All are silent. It is a heavy silence. They make me sick. It seems they don't even understand. What does Russia mean to this little cretin? They make me very sick indeed.

He's shaking with rage now. His tiny eyes stare at the prisoner, trying to transfix him. Then he jumps, and, in mid-air, punches the red-haired man in the face. A small blackish rivulet appears, glistening down from the lips to the chin of the red-haired man, but he doesn't say a word, just turns his head away with a pitiful frown.

Well, I couldn't care less, but this pugnosed little bastard makes me sick. I know the type. For them it's all the same what they're selling, whom they're selling, as long as they can go on living somehow.

So I yell across to him:

—Listen, you shitty assface, come on over here, I've got something to tell you!

A little obsequious smile appears on his dog's snout, as if to say, I know your tone, you're one of us . . . . He comes over, stopping before me, his feet well apart in chrome leather boots which obviously are too large for him.

—Now now, old bird, when did they let you out?

I don't even get up. I just kick him in the balls.

—There, you lump of shit! That's my address and my certificate of release, too! Now why don't you come over and see me sometime when you're feeling sort of lonesome?

Hiccupping and groaning he rolls on the ground, legs jerking spasmodically, for at least a minute. Then he gets up—on all fours, that is—and disappears.

A small, dry, more-cough-than-laugh comes over my shoulder:

—You're not scared?

I turn toward the voice. Two gray eyes, half-closed,

as if to protect themselves against the vivid light, are watching me with some irony and also with great seriousness.

—No.

And it's true, I have no reason to be afraid. From the S.S. people's point of view my biography is impeccable. That feeble creature wouldn't dare to squeal on me: he knew with whom he had been dealing . . . .

—Where did you do yours?

—What are you—questioning me or something?

—Don't get me wrong, what I mean is, maybe we've been places together.

—Doesn't seem so to me, old man. Haven't seen you on my travels . . . .

—Maybe you haven't been looking.

—The Dalstroï?

—That's more like it.

—How long?

—Seven. And you?

—Two years.

—So that's it! You're a thief?

—Yes, I am a thief. And you, daddy, they probably ran you in for sheer saintliness and light?

—Article 58, paragraph 11.*

—I see.

—What do you see?

—Just about everything.

—Now it could well be that you don't see anything

---

* Relates to "aiding the world bourgeoisie."

at all. If you want to know, I was captured half-dead, and that's the only way they could ever get me. You have a look at this!

He pulls up his tunic. His shirt, tight against his skin, is all the dressing his wounds have. He is covered with streaks of clotted blood. I sigh, in sympathy:

—Yes . . . .

But then I tell him straight:

—But then, you politicians are the worst lot, as a rule . . . .

—That's what you think?

—I know it.

—Then you don't know much.

—I've seen them, old man.

—You've never seen a real politician.

—What's the difference? Everybody is the same anyway: bastards all!

—What a way to speak of mankind!

—Shitdiggers!

—According to you I'm one, too?

—You're one, all right . . . .

—If that is all we are, why did you come to the help of that officer?

—I didn't do it as a favor to him. I just didn't like that other creepy mug.

—You're just another bastard, my son.

—I am what I am, yessir.

We go on insulting one another, dispassionately, for quite some time. And in the days after that, on the march, we come back to this conversation again and again. I can't really get the better of this damn furrier. His life hasn't been any easier than mine, it's been tougher, if anything. With his words, violent like exploding mines, he makes me lose confidence in myself:

—You accuse men? But have you been living among *men?* You believe real men to be the same as the scum you've known. Your Albert Ivanovitch was simply a Czarist officer who got away with it, his brain probably half rotten with syphilis anyway . . . . You can't stand those in power? Is a jailer, a turnkey, your idea of the power of the Soviet Union? I've been there too, I've been in jail, and I know it isn't sweet. But after seven years there were people who went to the trouble of seeking me out—of taking up my case, of getting me acquitted and rehabilitated! I'm no big shot, I'm a simple furrier. But, so there *are* good men, so there *is* justice! And you ask me why I enlisted: well then, I enlisted because it is my country, my own country I can feel under the soles of my feet.

Speeches, and in my lifetime I've heard more than my share of them. Words like wind in your ears. But what is there behind them? It is true that with this furrier the speeches seem to take on body, a tangible quality; he puts the truth of his life across in them, and I defend myself against them with all the fury accumulated in years of wolfish life.

During the halts Uncle Vanya always comes to rest beside us. Lying down, always "at attention," he eagerly absorbs all our talk. From time to time, usually at the most heated moments, a mocking smile glints through his swollen eyelids; and going by that it is easy to see that Uncle Vanya does not believe in my words any more than in Semyon Semyonovitch's. Maybe he too has his own truth and conceals it in himself and keeps it to himself. Perhaps life provides every one of us with a part of truth at our moment of birth . . . .

We are driven from camp to camp, along smoking roads and through the furnace heat of July noons. The roads coat our teeth with gritty dust, and this sends shivers down our spines. We are coughing up these roads again, with a dry, lung-rending cough. We march through towns and villages, and they all look flattened and squat, as if crushed by these atrocious times. The women who watch us pass look dark, distressed and mute, like tombstones.

They leave food and drink for us by the roadside. Often we can see their tubs full of water from a long distance away, and, coming up closer, small bundles lined up against the tubs and looking like rows of many-colored birds. We know for certain that we can never reach these, but each one of us is tearing the bundles apart in his imagination, grabbing the foodstuffs, gorging himself . . . . The most tempting and essential thing is water. All thoughts in our heads reduce themselves to a single desire: to drink! What wouldn't I give for a swig of water! This thirst gets so overwhelming that I sometimes feel metamorphosed into a dried stockfish, hanging out in the sunglare. As the head of our column passes the big tub, the crackle of a submachine gun tears through the dead hot silence. Dozens of eyes turn to stare at the glittering jets of water now escaping from the boards: They disappear, are sucked up into the earth, into its countless crevices; with every little wrinkle the scalding earth absorbs them almost immediately . . . . During the next few minutes nothing is heard but the irregular patter of hundreds of bare feet on the hot dust, and this murderously calm, trickling sound.

It is the Bald One who perforates the tubs, an old NCO who marches guard on our flank. He looks surprisingly like a turkey cock: a huge Adam's apple bobs constantly up and down in his stiff, long neck, and this supports a narrow, egg-shaped death's-head with prominent, bony brows. There is a steady, tranquil, one might almost say good-humored look in his eyes. He never raises his voice, he never beats you. He simply shoots to kill. He does his shooting in a workmanlike, German manner, and he has probably liquidated more than half of the prisoners that have fallen by the roadside.

I give the furrier a surreptitious nudge, nodding toward the Bald One:

—Have a look at that specimen of the human race, you truth-lover . . . .

Without turning his head the furrier hisses his reply through clenched teeth:

—It would be more useful if you'd figure out how many women have had to work together to prepare those bundles and bring them here—for you, you damned idiot!

The submachine gun spouts hot lead at the end of our

column. Again, one less. We go on, marching, marching to the west.

But now one among us raises a wild yell:

—Brothers—*a cloud!*

All heads turn toward the horizon, and true enough: a bluish black cloud, heralding thunder and rain, hangs there in the bleached pale sky. The same question rises into all our eyes: Will it come this way, or will it pass us by? To begin with, the rain is just a mean little sprinkling in the dust. The water drops strike our heat-tanned faces like small fiery sparks. Then again nothing, silence, only our hearts beating wildly, whipped on by hope. Then, a whirlwind, making the dust swirl from one side of the road to the other; and it opens the floodgates, it is a tremendous, noisy downpour, striking the column slantwise. We offer it our heads, our eyes, our mouths, we are more than willing to get drenched in it! Semyon Semyonovitch tears off his tunic, it is heavy and swollen with rain:

—Use your hands, Seryosha, drink!

My palms wring out a mixture of July clouds and earth dust and human blood, cup it to my mouth, and I drink, drink, almost choking myself. Uncle Vanya is wringing out the hems of the shirt he wears plastered to his body, catching the liquid in his other hand and licking the moisture off his palm like a dog. The bald-headed German keeps on marching by our side with measured step, small wrinkles of gloom in the corners of his mouth. You can't exterminate the rain by shooting it.

It is still pouring at nightfall, as we lie down close together, back to back. And the next morning I wake up to those only-too-familiar jitters . . . .

I try to tell myself that they are only caused by the cold, that they'll be gone by midday. But the cramped feeling in my jaw, the sour taste in my mouth tell me otherwise, giving the diagnosis: the old malaria. In these circumstances, any sickness, however insignificant, means death. And this isn't just any sickness, it is the malaria. When we are given orders to get up and start out again, I know for certain that I'm as good as gone. The road, the people, everything dissolves into a kind of flickering mist.

Semyon Semyonovitch takes my arm and shakes it, looking worried:

—What's the matter with you, Sergei? You have to keep going. Get a grip on yourself, come on! But how you look, brother—what is wrong with you?

—Malaria!

—I see . . . . Now listen, son, you ever try to get on the subway after a tremendous drunk? The problem is as simple, here. You've got to stay as firmly on your two feet as possible, so that bald devil doesn't get a chance to line his sights up on you! I'll try to prop you up, son, if you'll keep going till tonight, everything will be fine, you can rest there and tomorrow you'll be fit again. Now let's go!

And I am marching again, though hardly able to lift my leaden feet. My head is full of a dull, tinkling sound, and there are circles, circles, circles forming and dancing in front of my eyes . . . . They multiply, float about in chains, explode in rainbow-tinted splodges, fall like heavy hail.

Semyon Semyonovitch is supporting me with his bony shoulder, careful not to let the guard notice anything. Well, that is something. Worth more than all the speeches he's given me . . . .

Thirst, thirst, hellish thirst . . . . As if someone had crammed my lungs with burning coals, like the innards of a samovar. A harrowing fire has been lit inside me, demanding water and still more water. I pass a leathery tongue over my lips:

—Water!

Semyon Semyonovitch's voice reaches me through a thick mattress of hot air:

—Be patient, Seryosha, try to keep going! As soon as that bald son-of-a-bitch is relieved, I'll try to dip my tunic into the ditch. Now I can't even try!

But I can't stop myself from repeating it over and over again, that single word:

—Water, water, water . . . .

All at once Semyon Semyonovitch is moving away from me.

—Wait a minute—try to keep on going, straight on! The bald devil seems to have gone over to the other side of the column . . . .

Within hardly a second a short burst explodes almost beside my ear, returning me for a moment to my full senses. I see Semyon Semyonovitch broken in two, falling awkwardly onto his knees, then trying to break the fall with his elbow, and finally sliding into the ditch, turning over on his back. And my memory goes blank again.

I do not know how I got through that day. My senses return to me in the middle of the night. Cold, unblinking stars are sprinkled across the depths of an inky black sky. The guards are talking, cracking jokes, laughing. Uncle Vanya lies by my side, at full attention as usual; his almost dead eyes are watching me like questioning half-moons. Then comes his voice, in a rapid whisper:

—A minimum of exertion, a minimum of emotion. The law of the conservation of energy . . . .

I feel like shouting back at him, something strident and deafening, to pierce him through and through. But I can't think of anything, not even of some dirty crack about his mother.

11

~~~~~~

The first thing I know upon waking is the sun, masses of sun, sharp and blinding winter sunshine. It comes slanting in through the thawing spots on the window-panes, illuminating the churning of a myriad of luminous particles in the air. The room is empty, but there is a hoarse, cold-stopped voice giving orders in the corridor.

—Now the most important thing I need, Simotchka, is a lot of steaming hot water, as much of it as possible. I have to thaw out my hands first—if they don't work properly, nothing will. My god, they feel like bone all the way through. When did they bring him here?

71

—Three days ago. Nikolai found him down there, on the taiga.

—Who knows how long he dragged himself along out there . . . . His temperature?

—Hundred point four this morning.

—Does he complain?

—He doesn't say a thing. He is very tough. The only thing he wants to know is whether his legs are going to be cut off or not.

—But still, his pains must be infernal. Where does he come from?

—No papers on him, I suppose he must be a member of some expedition.

—Anyway, that isn't very important right now. Does he take food?

—Hardly anything.

—That's understandable. Simotchka, will you get everything ready for me. We'll try to turn this lad into a first-class ballroom hero yet!

—May God hear your words!

There are steps, drawing nearer now. Measured, resilient steps. I close my eyes, pretending to sleep. The floorboards in my room are creaking now, and somebody seats himself quietly on the stool beside my bed. Thick, cold fingers, they seem still drenched with wind and snow, encircle my wrist, making me aware of my own pulse-beats. The man sitting beside me smells of cheap tobacco and sheepskin. I raise· my eyelids surreptitiously. I see a colossal man, about thirty-five, massively built, his face pitted with pockmarks, a short doctor's tunic pulled over his faded jacket. He is attentively following the second hand ticking away on the face of his watch, his heavy jaw muscles in light motion under the pitted skin. So that's you, I think, Ivan Antonovitch! He puts the watch back into his pocket, gives me a penetrating stare:

—You're not asleep?

—No. I'm not.

—Are you in pain?

—Will you operate on me?

—That is my intention.

—An amputation?

—We'll see.

—I won't let you cut my legs off.

—Are you afraid?

—I lost that habit when I was a child. But it is better to be put away in a wooden box than to go on living without one's legs.

—Are you a dancer?

—Haven't tried it yet.

—You'll get a chance . . . .

Ivan Antonovitch gets up. He is large and thickset like a bear. There is a mocking expression in his half-closed eyes.

—Well then! Fasten your seat belt, we're off.

He goes out of the room.

—Sima, are you ready?

—Five minutes, Ivan Antonovitch.

I hear the front door go, feel a puff of icy air coming into the room. Then:

—Ivan Antonovitch—you didn't meet him?

The doctor lowers his voice as far as that kind of voice can be lowered.

—No, Galya, we didn't meet.

—Perhaps you passed without seeing each other?

—Yes, that's it. Our routes must have crossed.

—Did you come by the Ravine of the Wolves?

—By the Ravine of the Wolves, Galya.

—But that is the way he said he was going too . . . .

—Galynka, my darling, you know it yourself—the taiga isn't like any old avenue in Irkutsk . . . .

Sima's voice puts an end to this gloomy dialogue.

—Silovna, fetch the water.

The old woman's voice comes from the other end of the corridor, from another world:

—I'm coming.

—Get him ready, Sima.

The restful confidence of that hoarse deep voice is inspiring, and I start hoping for the best. I'll get to Shatsk yet. To keep all other thoughts out I close my eyes again and start counting: "one . . . two . . . three . . . ." When I reach one hundred, I start over again. "One . . . two . . . three . . . ." But then I am lifted up from my bed and transferred to another resting-place. It seems hard and cold.

In spite of my drowsiness I can still hear the voices whispering:

—Take care, Silovna. Now hold his left leg. That's it. Cover him up.

—He's got no weight to him at all!

—Skin and bones.

"Nineteen, twenty, twenty-one . . . ." I am wheeled away; then we stop, and a hoarse voice is talking to me from above.

—We'll start in a minute. Can you hear me?

Silently, I nod, without interrupting my count: "forty-seven, forty-eight, forty-nine . . . ." The last thing I hear is a staccato exchange, reminding me of a rollcall:

—Ready?

—Ready.

—Mask.

—Here.

—Anesthetic.

—Starting.

"Ninety-three . . . ninety-four . . . ninety-five . . . ."

12

~~~~~~

The train hiccups and jumps at each joint of the rails. The car window cuts a rectangle of darkened and almost impenetrable shadow out of the night, vague human shapes are reflected within it. Without the intermittent shocks from the wheels of the train nothing would indicate that we are moving. Above the compartment door the small yellow splotch of the conductor's lantern looks like an oscillating glowworm, and in the murky reflection faces seem gray and shadowy. I'm lying under a seat, my head turned toward the corridor, surrounded on all sides by human bodies and baggage. Above me there is a little inferno of moans and whispers and curses, and always one word, short and rough like the crack of a whip, repeating itself throughout the carriage. You can hear it pronounced in all sorts of ways and shades of meaning, at times bitterly, at times ruminatively, and at times almost vindictively. It weeps, it sighs, it becomes raucous and drunken, finally it dissolves into voluptuous giggles. It takes away your breath and coats your gums with sour spittle. I have known this word since I was a child, but I never realized it could contain so many meanings.

—Some bread.

—The bread.

—The drought.

—Spring will be very hard.

—We'll go begging.

—Disaster.

—Now we've gotten through the war, we're faced with famine.

—The main thing is not to get panicky.

But in another corner the subjects are different:

—Now have another!

—She's great.

—We're all right . . . .

Involuntarily, I turn round to look. I can feel my ravenous hunger contracting all muscles, up to my cheeks: because there are two, *eating*—cramming themselves behind the shelter of their sleeves, their eyes flickering round like the eyes of burglars on the job . . . . The one sitting in front of me has a spongy, damp face, surrounded by a sparse beard growing in scattered tufts all over his sagging cheeks. He doesn't seem to use his teeth at all, his flabby, old-womanish lips seize the morsels gently, noiselessly. I can't tear my eyes off him. I am fascinated by that piece of bread, it excludes all other thoughts. A hard piece of bread, surrounded on all sides by that loose-lipped mouth. Our eyes meet. Slowly he puts his feet down on the floor again: they are covered with rags fastened around the ankles with safety pins. A nauseating stench of sour sweat penetrates my nostrils.

I feel dizzy. Everything begins to turn in front of my eyes, all objects lose consistency and definition. Close by my ear a conversation in rapid whispers.

—You shift over a little—come on, have another bite, don't be afraid. It isn't stolen . . . . Tell me, where are you going? Come on, have some more . . . . I can wait . . . . You're a strong guy . . . .

—What's the use of being strong?

—I'm the head, you be the arm. We could feed together, we'd be better off that way . . . .

—Doing what?

—You just give me a hand—that's all.

—Listen, I'm not strong for that kind of work.

—All you have to do is pick up as much as you can and then make off with it, as far as you can go.

—Aah, go to hell!

—Well, well—if you're that proud, you can go on sucking your thumb!

At that moment a whispered warning comes floating through the car, reaching my ears:

—The militia . . . the militia . . . .

And that is another word which can be pronounced in a great variety of ways . . . . The drunkard's whisper has stopped. From where I am I can see a man approaching through the carriage, negligently stepping over the prostrate bodies and sacks, heading straight toward me. In this jumble of close-packed human beings he looks almost gigantic, enormous, full of authority in the way he walks, in the way his big eyes look out of his big, broad face. He carries a kerosene lamp in one hand, throwing light into the dark corners, and his right hand rests on the holster on his belt. Now he is blocking out the light from above. A rubber-covered boot, still damp, looms large before my eyes. The light of the lantern becomes stronger and stronger.

—Hey! You down there, let's have a look at you.

My neighbor, shivering and cursing in an almost inaudible voice, emerges first. The voice resounding above my head becomes maliciously amused.

—Now now, greetings! You know me from the photo . . . . Isn't it amazing, my dear little Khizhniak, what an enormous family you have! But you see, you can't just go on grazing off the whole of the Soviet Union to feed all your offspring. Oh, I see, you've even hired a servant, it seems? One might say you're traveling with all your staff, hey? Come on out, you good servant you, if you please! Not bad, not bad at all—the old slave trader has good taste . . . . Good-looking kid. You had him for long?

I cut into his rambling:

—I'm not his man!

He looks at me, blinks as if the light were too strong, playing games with his badly focussing eyes. He can't be more than four years older than me, maybe five.

—Well, where do you come from, then?

He is obviously a man with both feet planted firmly on the ground. Suddenly I have a desperate need to say a few words to him, no matter what, to get some sign of comprehension from him, a look or a gesture, to get a small fraction of his strength and assurance transferred to myself. But my stubborn lips cannot frame more than these brief words:

—From captivity.

His convex eyes light up. He says, now in a completely different tone of voice—perhaps spiteful, perhaps troubled?—giving me a light shove to move in front of him:

—All right, we'll take you along, we'll see. Agureyev, you take that one. Now don't get so terribly worried about those old rags of yours, Khizhniak. One might say you don't really need them any more, those rags . . . .

The sergeant, sleepy fish-eyes above a flattened nose, escorts me to the platform at the end of the car. He throws a look over his shoulder, opens the door, stands beside it:

—Go ahead, go ahead—jump!

—Why should I?

—You know how it is, these days . . . . Guys like you are none too welcome anywhere. Jump, or you'll land in a lumber camp!

I can't make up my mind. Somehow I want to stay: that man in his boots and goloshes would understand my grief, my tribulations, he could help me escape from this infinite chaos in which I have been floundering for so many years. I trust him, I trust him in spite of all the bitter experiences I have had with men . . . .

But this one, the sergeant, is still pushing me toward the door, ever so gently, and as my feet touch the threshold, I jump out into the night. The rumbling earth flies up to meet me.

13

~~~~~~~~~~~~~~~~~~~~~~~~~~~~~~

I wake up to a monotonous mumbling beside my bed. Silovna sits on the stool, and the tip of her nose, rough like pumice, moves up and down below the bridge of her old-fashioned spectacles.

There is a sheet of paper in her hands, covered in longhand on both sides; her flabby lips are busily catching and enunciating the words that seem to escape and slither all over the place.

—And then, to end this letter, we would like to tell you that we have sent you three hundred rubles. We hope that you will buy yourself something you like, for the feast. My wife Nyura and my son Styopka send their regards. I remain your loving son, Pyotr. I almost forgot to tell you, I have been promoted to foreman, and we will soon get lodgings of our own . . . .

I make a cautious attempt to move my legs—and a joyful thought seeps into my consciousness: I still *have* my legs! I am still in possession of my legs! I can still walk this terrestrial globe on my very own legs! A dizzying sense of weightlessness engulfs me; but I still doubt my luck, I have to ask the old woman:

—Tell me, mother, is it true that I still have my legs . . . ?

—Your legs? Why of course, darling, of course! And why shouldn't you? Ivan Antonovitch never fails in his operations! Do you know, they promised him an appointment to Novosibirsk, they wanted to give him a professor's chair, and his own apartment, and everything—but he, he didn't want to go! He's in bed now with a bit of a temperature, after that long walk here yesterday . . . . Forty versts in a blizzard like that!

—And, tell me, this other—Sima, isn't that her name?

—Oh, Sima, she'd never leave him!

—They don't have any children?

—Oh my, that's quite a story. You know, and this is a fact, they're not a couple at all. Of course Sima, she'd love to have him, she adores him with all her heart, but our Ivan Antonovitch, he's married, he has a family in Irkutsk. But his wife has ideas of her own, she doesn't want to move away from there. And he's been with us for at least twelve years . . . . Sima has been in love with him ever since they were in the front lines together.

Well, that's the way she is. Her heart is the size of thirty-three princesses, but she isn't all that beautiful . . . .

—Do I have stay in bed for a long time yet, do you know?

—What difference does that make to you? You stay here, put on a little weight, why hurry? How could you ever do any honest work in the state you're in now! But if you want to send word to someone, we can do that for you, we can notify your parents, or write to your superiors . . . .

—No, that isn't necessary. I mean . . . .

—Now, don't be so cocky. You know, my son, my little Pyotr, he always writes me, no matter if there's a sad story to tell or a happy one! You see, he's just sent me a letter, a registered letter too . . . . He's a fisherman at Murmansk. Our family have always been fishing people, from way back. And I've been very fortunate with my daughter-in-law, she's given me two little grandchildren, boys, both of them. And he tells me they've now sent me some money, but that isn't important, it's just that they don't ever forget me. You wouldn't believe, but sometimes when I haven't heard from them I start sorting out their old letters and read them again, and every single one of them is as beautiful as a song . . . .

Her own words become a sing-song, monotonous lullaby, calming and wearying me. My thoughts have already begun to move far away from this room with its snow-covered windows, with its thin curtains . . . . From now on, I'll have to use every quiet moment for serious calculations, hard thinking! If I want to go the full distance, I've got to figure it all out, down to the smallest detail. In winter, it is almost impossible to leave a taiga village on the quiet, without being noticed. But it is just that little "almost" that I have to find. And I'll find it, I'll go. All I need is a really windy night . . . . My clothes must be somewhere in this house. And skis I can get hold of in any old shed; so I just need that good, wild wind, nothing else.

But it is almost grotesque: in these thoughts, turning around my impending liberation, a kind of muddled dissatisfaction with myself keeps intruding. It is as if, like that man with his twisted legs, the prisoner, I had to spit into somebody's heart without any reason at all. The wild-haired boy who went off with his dogs to get the doctor from the district town is still lost somewhere on the taiga. I try to fight against my weariness, I want to ask the old woman about this boy. But I have to fall—back into unconsciousness—and the question remains unspoken.

14

I couldn't help getting off at this station. Acting against the most elementary laws of the vagabond tribe, against all good sense, I am indeed getting off at this station! And here I am, standing on the station square, facing my home town, without really recognizing it. It is no more the Yuzhnogorsk of yesteryear, of the years before the war. Beyond the rustling acacia trees I can see the new thoroughfares of the new city, with its new houses, new colors, new smells.

At nightfall I am still rambling through unfamiliar streets, trying to find at least a trace, however small, of my childhood, scrutinizing the faces of people that pass. But at the crossings the utterly faceless streets of this town escape me; they run away in all directions, away from me. Only by Khytrovo pool do I hit upon a tiny island of the past. Forced almost to the water's edge by the impenetrable outside wall of a huge factory building, sunk into the ground to half its height, there is the little house of old Guryan the Blessed, its walls gone askew at all four corners. The roof of this house was my hiding place more than once as an escape from punishments and humiliations. The old man used to live there all by himself, oblivious to the world. For days on end he could busy himself making all sorts of toys for us little marmots of the suburbs, using as materials anything he could find on the town's dumping grounds . . . .

I go on knocking on this well-known door for a long while; then an old fat woman, wearing a greasy apron, comes to open it. A heavy kitchen smell escapes into the air and into my nostrils. She stares at me with a questioning look in her faded eyes, wipes her fingers on the apron.

—Please tell me, who is it lives here now?
—What do you mean—who lives here now?
She gives me a suspicious once-over.
—It's us, the Kashkin family. This is our house.
—Have you been living here for a long time?
—Yes, well, ever since Guryan the Blessed died . . . .
—I see . . . .
—But who are you? Are you one of his relatives? We

can show you all the legal documents, on the purchase of this house, and the certificate given by the town soviet too . . . .

Then, as I'm walking away, I hear her muttering:

—All sorts of people, coming here to stare . . . .

After that I take a long rest. I lie on the grass below the railroad embankment, the back of my head cushioned on my palms. I've stopped thinking. In fact, it seems to me now that there never was such a thing as my childhood in this town, that it was all a dream. There is no earthly evidence for it whatsoever; so, probably, there never was one.

The piercing whistle of a locomotive tears me out of my reveries. Above me, picking up speed slowly as it goes, a freight train rumbles by. I negotiate the embankment at top speed, and as the brakeman's step goes pitching by I grab hold . . . . Scrambling on I find myself face to face with a young man in his early twenties. He has a heavily freckled face, big round eyes, a most serious expression. He sits there on a pitiful little bundle, munching a slice of bread. He draws back, hospitably, and says:

—Have a seat. There's enough room here for both of us.

—So you're not going to chase me off again?

He breaks the bread and gives me half.

—How far you going?

—Well, one might say it's far . . . . One can't go much farther!

—Who knows, maybe we're both heading for the same place?

—Well, where are *you* going?

Stuffing his mouth with bread crumbs he lisps:

—To Angara. You've heard of it? My father is down there, I've never even met him. My mother tells me he disappeared, but how can she know for sure? He's probably gone where everybody's going, and everybody is going to Angara— just about everybody . . . .

—But man, that's a long way to travel.

—I'll get there. And I'll walk up to the boss, and I'll ask him: Where is Pal Palytch Gorobtsov working now? That's my father, Pal Palytch. So that makes me Sergei Palytch.

He goes on talking a mile a minute, passionately, with great conviction and incoherence; and I can't get down that little lump I suddenly find forming in my throat. What should I think, what should I say to this kid? Or is it that our poor human speech has no word for it? I put my hand on the boy's head, spreading all five fingers into his tangled wheat-yellow hair:

—Oh well, Seregya, Seregya, you'll end up in the claws of some Albert Ivanovitch! And then you'll find out what "Angara" means . . . .

The kid doesn't say anything. He is obviously trying to figure out whether there is any sense to what I've just said or not. Then, with a pensive frown:

—No, I won't fall into their claws.

The train is slowing down. The small, crisscrossed streets of a village and its station buildings are moving up to the railroad. I have to get off soon, if I don't want to get copped by the station police.

—Now you lie down, old man, I tell the kid.—And while the train is halting at the station, I'll go and get us some fuel for the journey. It's a long way to Angara!

The kid gives me a brothers-in-crime wink . . . .

I jump off at a stretch protected from sight by a narrow strip of trees, walk across to the highway and head back to the station, as if I was coming from the village. The depot looks deserted, except for a bewhiskered militiaman standing on the well-lit entry platform. Too late to blow retreat! He must have seen me. With the most assertive manner I can muster I walk toward a sales kiosk. As I am discussing matters with the saleswoman, I can feel his persistent gaze at the back of my neck: he is scrutinizing me. I start asking for one thing, then switch over to another, to stave off what is, by now, inevitable . . . . The pencilled eyebrows of the saleswoman, a smart and matronly person, move steadily upward to express her amazement at such an extremely hard-to-please customer. When finally, loaded down with all sorts of foodstuffs, I decide to call it a day and turn around, the militiaman has advanced to a distance of about five steps from me. He is really trying his best to look formidable. Now it will all be over in a couple of seconds. I take a step in his direction, and my dried-up mouth opens to express the first thought that enters my head:

—Listen, sergeant— there's a tiny little kid riding that train. I think you should collect him now, he might end up God knows where . . . .

Instead of answering, the whiskers salute me.

—Where?

Now this is what I call plain sailing. Over there, in the shadowy spaces between the boxcars, it will be easier to get away than here. This is open ground. But we start marching along the train, and all the way I sense the short, inquisitive glances of the militiaman. The inspectors' tools move over the car trucks with a metallic, jerkily clicking sound. I stop by the brakeman's platform:

—This is it.

The sergeant takes his torch switches it on.

—Get up, dear comrade, we've arrived!

The kid sits there, blinking in the cruel light that glares into his face. Then he gets up, without saying a word, and descends obediently with the sergeant. His eyes meet mine for an instant, and with an anger and contempt anything but childlike he snarls at me:

—So much for you!

I am so surprised I forget my act: crackers, pastries, sweets slip from my grasp and fall, rolling all over the place. The sergeant salutes me again.

—And you, citizen, I have to ask you to accompany me to the station, to give a statement.

Thinking fast, I force myself to reply calmly, in an almost offhand manner:

—But you see, comrade sergeant, I'm rather pressed for time—why don't you just do the good deed and leave me alone . . . .

An empty car is slowly rolling by; gathering all my strength I jump, grab the upper edge of the car, swing myself on top and jump down again on the other side.

—Halt— halt— I warn you, I'll shoot!

Sounds like children's firecrackers exploding behind me . . . . Diving under the carriages I rush toward the lights on the other side of the tracks, but then something, somebody comes tumbling down on top of me, forcing me to the ground in a stranglehold. I am choking, I hear my own voice rattling out of my mouth:

—Leave me alone, you bastard! I'll go with you.

15

~~~~~~

Sleep is receding, but I keep my eyelids closed. For the
time being I rely more on my ears than on my eyes, I
file away every chance word in my memory, like a miser
hoarding his coins; each one of them might signify my
death, or my recovery, or some important news— or it
might be a danger signal, or good tidings . . . .

Also, I am afraid of being diverted from my aims.

In the corridor, by the door, Sima is trying to console
Galya. Galya is in tears.

—In your condition, my little dove, one just can't let
oneself go like that. You shouldn't think only of yourself, just now.

—But it isn't myself I am thinking of!

—Well then, it isn't a needle we have to find again, but a man. And he'll be found. All the men of the neighborhood have gone out to search for him, they're going through the taiga with a fine comb—and they've got reindeer with them, they've sent out the helicopters, and you are crying as if all this would be done for nothing, for a dead man! Are your tears going to be of any help to anyone? Listen, your Nikolai is sitting by a stove in one of those winter huts, and he'll be all right.

—But it's just that I haven't even told him . . . .

—And a good thing, too! When he comes back, that piece of news is going to please him even more! And I'll be your godmother. Oh, come on now, you little fool, why can't you stop, at least for a moment, why don't you go in there and sit down by his side for a while, we'll have to give him his serum soon . . . .

Sima's steps are retreating down the corridor. They sound slow and heavy. The little nurse with the high cheekbones comes in, sits down on the stool beside my bed. I feel her gaze on my face, a steady, inquisitive, hostile gaze. But whereas all hostility, no matter from whom, has always been deflected by the impenetrable wall of my own hatred, I feel less secure now. I know I am no better than the smallest of small-time gamblers who refuses to pay a debt. My whole philosophy has been shaken and cracked throughout its length and width. Faces, faces, I am surrounded by faces, I can see them. The faces of people I have met in all kinds of tight corners . . . . The big-eyed militiaman on the night they arrested my father; Semyon Semyonovitch; Seryoshka on the brakeman's platform; Nikolai, the wild-haired boy who went out into the blizzard; these hospital people . . . . I have been arguing with them all my life, and it is too late to turn about. My life has been lived. It is impossible to start all over again. I'll go, I'll just go, and I'll tread on their faces if necessary.

The girl is still watching me, she is watching me all the time, as if she could read my thoughts. I can't stand it any longer.

—*I didn't ask him to go!*

—What is it? What—

—I didn't ask him to go, do you hear me? And don't stare at me, I don't like people staring at me.

—Very well, I won't do it again. But please, don't get excited now.

—What do you care if I'm excited or not, why are you trying to shut me up? I'll calm myself all right, all by myself! Get out, I'm telling you, just get up and go . . . .

—But what have I done to you?

—Leave me alone, do you hear me? I want to get some sleep, see? Go on, leave me alone, just leave me alone . . . .

She jumps up and runs to the door, then turns round with horror in her face; and I go on shouting, I shout and shout.

16

~~~~~~~~~~~~~~~~~~~~~~~~~~~~~~~~~~~~~~~

I push a dry larch tree stump into the campfire, to get it started. A swarm of sparks flies up and away into the taiga night. Small flames appear under the stump, licking upward on the dry bark. The darkness recedes, the roots of the trees around us become visible, and this man they call the Phonograph sleeping on my anorak. Ziama is sitting on the other side of the fire, resting his chin on his bony knees. Little yellow fire devils are dancing about in his eyes. I know what he is thinking. I got wise to it today, when we were looking for a ford to cross a river. Ziama looked at the village sprawling on the other side with such naked longing for warmth and comfort, that I knew there was no doubt about it. He was scared, he wouldn't go much farther. Why on earth had I burdened myself with him?

At the labor camp they respected Ziama for his mild-mannered ways and for his long, impassioned stories; he invented them himself. I had that in common with him, an interest in books. I had read a lot—one might even say a tremendous amount, considering the kind of life I've been leading. It is true that I only read out of curiosity. It is interesting to watch other people's lives unfold, even when you can't believe everything that's been written about them. Every book has its own subject, every one of them contains its own truth. Well, in real life it is much simpler; what's the use of pretty words in real life? As far as I'm concerned all of it can be expressed in this very, very simple formula: "Even the roast chicken wanted to live . . . . "

But Ziama's approach to books was different. He treated them like a believer treats his holy relics. For Ziama, a book is a guide to take him through the maze of life, and he is crammed with ideas. I'd say his mind is like a head of cabbage, every leaf an idea.

—Don't you see, he tells me—a good book contains all the experiences of a whole generation. Thanks to literature, humanity is advancing, in a kind of geometrical progression. You know, your attitude to books is very narrow, it's a consumer's attitude. And it seems to me that it might be better not to read anything at all, in these circumstances . . . .

As soon as I arrived in the labor camp I started making plans for escape. First of all I started watching and studying the others, looking for a buddy, a man who wouldn't be afraid of anything.

Slowly, I go through all my companions in the hut. But all these guys seem to be pretty gutless, loud-mouthed as some of them are. They don't inspire confidence. Finally I settle for a real tough character, a professional burglar, from the capital. His name is Nikolai the Phonograph, and he's a small, squat, dog-snouted type. He's a gloomy, stupid man, but the important thing about him is that he's utterly alone, like a finger sliced off a hand. And this seems very important to me; he has nothing to lose. It is impossible to get across the taiga without a buddy; the taiga wasn't made for hermits. That I have known ever since I was first sent up to one of these camps.

We make our plans, Nikolai and I. His share in the planning business is rather limited, just an impressive clenching of the jaws and a brief, hissing "yup" to anything I say.

Ziama turns up the night before we intend to leave.

—Take me with you, Sergei. I know you're going. But why don't you say something, why aren't you talking to me? Take me with you, I can't stand it any more . . . .

—Are you crazy?

—If I stay here alone, I will go mad, yes.

Somewhere deep down something starts vibrating, a kind of long-lost sympathy for the likes of Ziama, this small-time forger who has become so attached to me.

And while I know that he'll be a dead weight to be dragged along on this long trek, a heavy and dangerous ball and chain, I hear myself saying:

—If you say a single word on our way out, I'll wipe you off the earth!

Ziama's hand touches my elbow, and I can feel its feeble, yet grateful squeeze in the darkness.

The fire is burning low, and I push the larch stump in again, charred as it is. Ziama raises his palm to shield his face from the sparks.

—What are you thinking about, Ziama? I ask him in a low voice.

—What did you say?

—I was asking you for your thoughts . . . .

—Oh, nothing. I just remembered my mother. She used to work as a housekeeper at a school. Pretty hard work, too.

—What's the use of that?

—She always said: "Ziama, you'll come to a sticky end!" And you know, my mother must have been a pretty intelligent woman . . . .

—Don't think so much, Ziama, don't worry so much. All this thinking business is a kind of luxury anyway, and even more so out here on the taiga.

—But I can't stop myself from thinking, funny as it may seem to you. Really, is it possible that people live their lives without ever having a thought?

—Ziama, sometimes you give me the creeps. You

know, even the worst blockheads have nerves. I can't really take all this black magic at bedtime. Why don't you just go to sleep? It would do you more good than all this crap.

—But I don't want to sleep! I can't understand it myself, but I'm not at all tired. You know, I really envy you. I was never able to go away, anywhere, strange as it may seem: I, a forger, had to live all my life within my official identity . . . . With mother sick, where could we have gone? We always stayed right there, under militiamen's eyes . . . .

—Get some sleep, Ziama. You'll have time enough to remember your old lady. We have to get going at daybreak, there's no time to lose. Just think what might happen if snow starts falling before we're there! Go on, wrap yourself up and get some sleep.

—All right, I'll try, though I don't know if it's any use . . . .

He covers himself with his prisoner's jacket, lies down on his side. As he is dozing off I hear him muttering:

—Yes, it's true, I'll come to a bad end.

He falls asleep almost at once, his hands wedged between his small bony knees, like a child.

That will be his last sleep. I have no choice. If ever I let him go, he'll attract attention to our tracks, voluntarily or otherwise. It's me or him. I shouldn't have taken him along. I don't know why I've kept hoping that he'd have enough strength to get at least to the point where we agreed to go our separate ways. Yes, it is his last sleep. But as I am looking at this tiny figure of a man, bundled up in his cotton-wadded jacket, I can't get the better of a strange and repugnant weakness that makes itself felt in my hands. I go over and jostle him, gently. Slowly he turns over from one side to the other, murmuring in a nasal voice. Then he gives a start, rises on one elbow and says in a sleepy voice:

—That you, Sergei?

I can't even meet his eyes. I get up, turn my back to him.

—Come on, we're leaving.

His voice becomes deep and full of anxiety.

—But where are we going, Sergei? It's still dark . . . .

—Get up! But leave your jacket here. You won't need it anymore.

I can hear him catching his breath, scrambling to his feet.

—But you're all wrong, Sergei, I—

We make our way through the shadows, heading against the wind blowing from the Yenisey River. I am taking him to the river. He is crying and moaning against my shoulder like a little boy.

—Don't do this to me, Sergei. My mother is sick, very very sick. And she has money saved up . . . .

—Don't you try to poison me, you little lump of shit! I don't want anything from you.

And as we arrive on the riverbank, I tell him:

—You go first.

I can't see his face, but from his incoherent whispering I can understand what goes on inside him at this moment. And suddenly I know I couldn't do a thing like that, I don't have the strength to do it.

Full of rage against myself, for this weakness, I can now feel something almost like hatred rising in me:

—Well, go on, walk, you piece of pestilence!

—Sergei!

—Walk!

His jerky footfalls are silenced somewhere ahead of me, in the dark.

I go back to our camp. The Phonograph has already made himself comfortable on Ziama's jacket, his legs crossed Oriental fashion. He stares into the fire, blinking incessantly, his canine jaws moving in the same steady rhythm. He is eating, the thief. Still chewing, he turns around:

—You've done him in?

—You keep your dirty trap shut!

The Phonograph's voice takes on a conciliatory, even obsequious tone.

—Know how you feel. I've had to go through it myself. One doesn't feel so hot afterward, oh no. It is a living soul, after all . . . .

I am shaken with satanic fury:

—Will you shut up, you goddamn asshole! What the hell do you know about *souls?* You're nothing but a lump of shit, a skinful of sewage— one more word from you, and I'll croak you!

The Phonograph decides to hold his tongue.

When I wake up I feel the old fever again. I don't

want to kid myself, it is plain as daylight, it is the old sickness of the marshes. I wrap myself up closer in my jacket.

In the gloomy light of this autumnal morning, the Phonograph's face looks even more bestial and sinister than usual. As if expecting good news he comes closer to take a look at me:

—You sick?

—It's nothing, we'll get going in a minute.

I try to get up, but a blinding white wall knocks me back, the taiga is turning over, and my head feels like an enormous, tolling globe, filled with gravel.

—Are you leaving me here?

—I don't want to catch your sickness . . . .

—You'll never make it alone. To be alone on the taiga means certain death.

—I'll have to try, it's still two to one against. Because if I don't go now, we'll both be rotting away here. What's to lose?

—You're a shit, Phonograph.

—Like everybody else.

—That's true enough.

—You'd have gone, too.

—Yes, I would have gone.

—So that's it . . . .

—All right, get lost.

—I'll leave Ziama's jacket with you. In case you make it after all . . . .

I wrap myself up from head to toe. The Phonograph starts walking to meet his death. There's nothing I can do to hold him back. Here, on the taiga, men are ruled by their instincts, and I would have done the same in his position. He could have finished me off, to get my loot; but he didn't dare, he was afraid—though not so much of me, not of Sergei Zarev, but of his notorious past.

As for me, everything now depends on this: will it start snowing soon? I close my eyes, and the scalding waves of delirium come rushing in, the waves from the steep shore crowned with three palm trees . . . .

On regaining consciousness I find myself lying by a heap of cold cinders. The Phonograph has gone, and Ziama's jacket with him . . . . I stare up at the sky with great indifference; clouds like torn sails are traveling across that sky, and through their wavering ragged rents, from a great height, frozen stars are contemplating the earth. They are cold, very cold.

17

~~~~~~

A shout wakes me up; but the door, slamming at the
end of the corridor cuts it off, and a long, heavy silence
descends, to separate me from all life, like a dome of
glass. There is a feeling of disaster in the air.

I start shouting, as loud as I can:

—Nurse!

No one answers.

—Nurse!

No reply. The silence becomes oppressive. Leaning
over, I place my palms on the floor, and exerting all my
strength I slide off the bed. I manage to crawl out into
the corridor. The silence pushes me onward, across the

threshold. At the end of it I open the frost-covered door. The glaring light stabs my eyes; then, gradually, objects, trees, men start taking shape against a background of blinding white. I can now see tiny, dark, human figures surrounding a team of dogs; they are coming closer, the snow is crunching under their shoes and paws. Beside the sled, sinking into the snow up to her knees with every step she takes, walks the girl with the cheekbones, bareheaded, without seeing anything that goes on around her. She is staring at a dark shape lying in the sled. She isn't weeping, she isn't crying, she is just staring at the sled.

And now I know the meaning of this silence. I know who is lying there. I want to put an end to this silence, it is as intolerable as a continuous, piercing scream. And I cry out, with grief, with shame, with the unspeakable:

—Aaaaaaaaahhhhhh . . . .

Hands reach out, pick me up, carry me back toward the warm air. I keep my eyes shut, I am afraid of seeing their faces. But each word I hear myself saying is like a stone rolling off my shoulders:

—I'm a runaway. My name is Zarev. Sergei Zarev. Sergei Alexeyevitch.